THE COWBOY'S ANGEL

THE COWBOY'S ANGEL

LAURAINE SNELLING

$\mathcal{P}$ROLOGUE

Sod house somewhere southwest of Fargo 1875

But Pa, don't want you to go."

Anson Stedman picked up his four-year-old son and hugged him close. "I will be home soon. You must take good care of your ma."

"I will, but don't want you to go."

Belle smiled up at her husband, the firelight glinting off the blond strands in her hair. "Pa will be home soon, Abel. We need to take care of the cow and chickens, or they might freeze."

"I keep the fire going." He slid to the floor and hugged Rusty, his best friend in all the world. "You take care of Pa now, you hear me?"

Rusty, named for his color, cocked his head, one ear standing up, one flopping forward. He kissed Abel's cheek and wagged his feathered tail so hard he created a breeze.

Belle stood in the circle of her husband's arm, as they both smiled at the antics of boy and dog. She didn't want Anson to leave either, but he needed to make a trip for the much-needed supplies. He had planned to go earlier but various trials kept him home until they were desperate, and even now a storm could hit any day.

"I don't want to go, but if I don't, we and our animals won't make it through the winter." He hugged Belle one more time and, heaving a sigh, settled his knitted wool cap on his head and his flat-brimmed felt hat over it. With the scarf she last knitted for him tucked around his neck and under his wool coat, he waved good-bye. "Now don't you go standing on the stoop. You keep that baby inside where it's warm." His smile brought a return one from his wife who, with one hand on her mountainous belly and the other on her son's shoulder, smiled bravely. "And keep that rifle handy. You know how to use it if you have to." Together mother and son moved to the window to watch him drive the wagon hitched to their remaining mule toward the sun showing half a disk above the horizon.

The thought of using the rifle against a two-footed intruder had not entered her mind until they had one sometime before.

"Hurry home," she whispered. "Dear God, please keep him safe."

CHAPTER I

Three weeks later
Two days before Christmas

When is Pa coming home?"

"Anytime now." Belle sucked in a deep breath. She looked at the calendar nailed to the bottom shelf on the wall of their sod house. She had marked off the days, every terrible slow day, even though she kept busy enough for two people. That was the only way she could handle the terror.

Anson was more than two weeks overdue. He should have been gone ten or eleven days at the most. But when the big storm hit, she prayed he would stay in Fargo where he was safe. When it lasted for three of the longest days of her life, she reminded herself that God could see through a storm and protect her Anson. "Thou art my rock and firm foundation. I will not be afraid." She repeated the verse over and over and had finally set it to a tune to hum and sing. Singing it seemed the only way she knew to keep from going crazy. The weather never had really let up after that, but for one sunny day that seemed to be a promise that the storms wouldn't last forever.

But that depended on one's definition of forever.

In one lull, she and Abel had brought the cow and the ten chickens from the sod barn to the lean-to she and Anson had added the summer before. That way she could manage to care for them.

1

Bringing in hay on the sled had taken much of an afternoon. At least Anson had prepared for winter storms by stringing a rope from the house to the barn. Like her, the cow was expecting any day.

"I should never have let him go," she reminded herself for the fiftieth time. As if she had had any choice in the matter. On the Dakota Territory plains in 1875, one did what had to be done, no matter what, if one wanted to stay alive. Winters were especially unforgiving. She'd heard tell that the wind drove some of the homesteaders outside to their deaths. After those three days of constant howling, screeching wind with no other adults around, she understood their desperation. But for her son and the baby she carried, she might have been tempted to do the same.

She added wood to the stove Anson had purchased in spite of her remonstrances that they couldn't afford it. While she kept the fireplace going for extra heat, she now cooked on the top of the woodstove. The stove was another thing to be thankful for since Abel could feed the woodstove more easily than the fireplace. In case he needed to.

"Lord, please bring Anson home soon." Digging her fists into her aching back, she tried to stretch and relieve the pain that came intermittently. So far she'd not given a name to the fear. Surely the pains were too soon.

"Ma?"

"Ja, Son."

"I'm hungry."

"Is it that time already?"

Abel nodded, the blond lock of hair falling over his forehead. He needed a haircut again. At least something around here besides her belly was growing.

"Did you look for eggs?"

He nodded and shrugged at the same time. Hens did not like to be moved, and not laying was their best revenge.

"When Tulip has her calf, we will have milk again."

"Ja, that is so." Belle brought the kettle of soup in from the box in the lean-to where she kept things cold. The skim of ice on top of the kettle was mute testimony to the cold even inside sod walls.

When she lifted the kettle to set it on the stove, a sharp pain started in her back and circled around the front, making her catch her breath. The baby was coming, no doubt about it now. When the soup was hot, she was not surprised that she no longer felt like eating.

At least she was as prepared as she could be. A folded cloth for a diaper, a knit wool soaker, a tiny gown and a strip of cloth to wrap around the baby's belly. Scissors to cut the cord and tiny ties for tying it off. Anson was prepared to serve as her midwife. Abel was too young. The packet was all wrapped and waiting.

The baby inside of her was not waiting. Over the next hours as the pains grew worse, she walked and gave Abel instructions to keep the fire burning. To melt water for the animals if the buckets of snow she'd brought in ran out. She only filled the line of buckets behind the stove half full so Abel could carry them. Good thing he took after his father in size and strength.

Almost Christmas and she was having a baby. Had Mary felt as she did right now? Was she afraid? At least she wasn't dealing with a Dakota snowstorm at the same time and she'd not been alone. She'd had Joseph there.

Belle and Abel sat in the rocking chair together, and as she read to him the Christmas story, somehow the words found their way around her heart, too.

When the pains grew too strong, she told him, "You sit here, and Ma will walk and be right back." She paced the room from end to end, and when the spasm passed, they finished the story with the shepherds going back to tell everyone they met what they had seen. "Be not afraid," the angels commanded.

When Abel's eyes fluttered, she tucked him into the pallet on the floor by the stove where he would be warmest.

"Ma, I love you."

"And I love you. If you wake up and it's cold, you get up and put wood in the stove, all right?"

"Where will you be?"

"Right here. But you might wake up before I do."

He nodded and snuggled down.

She unrolled her pallet from the bed that was too far from the heat on a night like this and laid it beside his. And walked. Terror tore at her mind while the birthing pains ripped at her body. Surely it had not been this bad when Abel had been born. She muffled a scream with her hand. *Oh God, I can't do this. Walk. I can't walk.* She staggered back across the room, stopping to lean against the bed-post, using her breathing to help control the onslaught. Pain, waves of pain. Her mind tried to drift off.

"Put wood in the stove. Put wood in the fireplace." If she did both, they would run out of wood more quickly. The stove would have to do. *Lord, what do I do? Anson, where are you? Why did you leave me? Just when I finally learned to care for you, is God taking you away?* Rage fueled one trip across the room. But it was not his fault he had to leave. She gritted her teeth, and when that wasn't suffi-cient, she clamped down on a piece of cloth.

You cannot fall down! You cannot fall down. Through the blur of pain, she filled the stove again, set the damper to make the wood last longer, and collapsed on the pallet. The coals in the fireplace blinked like eyes, evil eyes waiting to pounce. *God help me!*

CHAPTER 2

Halloo the camp. Can I come in?"

Jeremiah Jensen waited for a reply. He'd known too many people who got blasted entering a stranger's camp. The fire was burning low, but he could see a form lying near it.

A dog barked. But he didn't come far from the campfire.

"I just want to use your fire to get some warmth back in these bones." The dog barked again.

Jeremiah listened closely. No, that was not a warning bark. He dismounted and, rifle at the ready, walked closer, his horse following him.

"Are you all right?"

Surely the blanket-wrapped form moved. Beyond the fire he could see a wagon. As he drew nearer, he realized the wagon was now only a frame. It appeared someone had been using the bed for firewood. The dog barked again, this time moving between Jeremiah and the man on the ground.

"Easy boy, not planning on hurting you or him." Jeremiah kept up the singsong he used for animals of all kinds and sometimes humans, too. The dog whined. Jeremiah moved slowly toward the man that he could now see was wrapped in a quilt and moving.

"I come to help you."

"Thank God." The answer was so weak as to be almost blown away on the slight breeze.

"Call off your dog, so's I can come to you."

"Rusty—no. Down."

The dog dropped to his belly, keeping his gaze on the stranger. Had Jeremiah not been watching, he'd have missed the tip of the tail that moved side to side. "Rusty, good boy. That's it now, easy." He reached the man's side. "Name's Jeremiah Jennings, and I'm heading north to work on a ranch. Mean no harm to you." While he spoke gently, he reached out a hand and laid it on the man's shoulder. "Can I roll you over here so I can see you or sit you up or ...?"

"Anson S-Stedman. I ... I ... too weak."

"Are you wounded?"

"No. Sick."

Jeremiah kept one eye on the dog, who was bellying closer. "Is your dog the bitin' kind?"

"N-no. Just doing his best to help."

"I'm going to put some wood on that fire, see if we can get you warmed up some. How long you been down?" He reached a hand out to the dog and got a sniff and a wag. He stood and pushed two boards farther into the fire, where they flared immediately. "I see you been burnin' the wagon. Do you have any food?"

"Someone stole it. Figured I was dead."

Jeremiah found a sack of beans under a bag of oats. A cook pot lay overturned the other side of the fire. He went to his saddlebags and pulled out some jerky and hard tack, his traveling food. So far he'd found farms that allowed him to bed down in the barn and even provided a meal or two. He'd left Texas four weeks earlier to go work for the same rancher who also had a spread on the western edge of Dakota Territory. The northern ranch needed a new general manager and horse breaker. The storms up here in the north country had slowed him down. He should have been there by now.

He filled the kettle with snow to melt and set it on the edge of the fire then returned to the man. "Can you sit up?"

"Don't know."

"I see. I'll be right back." He pulled the saddle off his horse and tied him to a wheel on what used to be the rear axle. Then he dumped the saddle on the ground and untied his bedroll. "I'm goin' to pull you up against that if you can sit." When the man slid to the side, Jeremiah tucked the quilt and the bedroll around him. "Be right back." He returned with the sack of oats and laid that so Anson could use it more as a pillow. Had to get him warmed up. "Good. Now I'm melting some snow, and I found beans, but in the meantime I got some hardtack here that I can soak soft enough that maybe you can eat it."

Anson coughed, but his effort was so weak it hardly raised the quilt. Mucus slithered from the side of his mouth.

"Where you headed?"

"Home."

"And you took sick?"

A nod. The dog crawled in next to the man on the ground, licked his cheek, and laid his head on Anson's shoulder.

"Good boy. Come on, snow, let's get to melting here." Shame he didn't have real firewood. Spread the warm around some. He returned to the wagon and pulled another board off, shoving the end in the fire like the others.

He poured the melted snow water into his own tin cup and set it by the fire to warm. Why did everything take so blasted long? Keep talkin' to him. "You sure got a good dog there. How'd you keep the fire goin'?" He didn't wait for an answer but broke off a piece of bread and dropped it in the water, stabbing it with his knife to soak faster. When it was warm, he took it to his patient. "Here we go. I'm goin' to spoon this into your mouth." He held the spoon of what was now gruel to Anson's mouth, but when nothing happened, he paused. "Anson, you got to eat this. Nice and soft, warm. Come on, open your mouth."

Anson's eyes fluttered. Slowly he complied. But the liquid leaked out the side.

"Come on, man, you got to swallow."

Eyes of such sadness as to make his throat catch stared at him. "Save Belle."

"Where is Belle?"

Anson gathered himself. "W-west. Near river." He collapsed, as if those words took all his strength. "Rusty."

"You mean the dog could show me where you live?"

The faintest of nods.

"We'll get you strong enough, and we'll set out."

A faint movement of his head was all Anson could muster. "Baby." His eyes opened again, and Jeremiah watched the life fade away. He closed the man's eyes, shaking his head. "Sorry I didn't get here sooner. Lord God, what am I to do now? Can't bury the body, no animal here to carry him. How far away is home? You got to be lis'nin'. You said You do."

He melted more snow and watered his horse. Shared some of his jerky with the dog, likewise a piece of hard tack. But his gaze kept returning to the body on the other side of the fire.

Rusty sat by his master as if he knew there was no way to warm him and stared off to the west.

"Rusty dog, I promise you, we'll start out first light." What a way to spend the night before the night before Christmas.

CHAPTER 3

Christmas Day

Belle floated awake on the most amazing dream. At least she figured it must be a dream. She laid there, eyes closed. No pain. Something moved next to her side. Eyes wide, she moved her head just enough to see a baby all wrapped and snuggled up to her side. Moving her head slightly, she realized she could see the fireplace at the end of her feet. No mountainous mound. Hadn't she decided not to add more wood to the fireplace, instead saving wood?

A clatter of the stove lids, and she saw Abel settling the lids back in place. He had replenished the stove. And the fireplace? Had she birthed and wrapped her baby and cared for herself without knowing? How could that be? She shut her eyes again, allowing herself to float back into her dream. A man had come. Who? Anson came home? She mentally shook her head. Abel would not be tending the stove were his pa here. But who and where was the man now?

His hands—he laid his hands on her belly, and with a wrench, the baby moved. The pain of it only teased the edges of her mind. No matter how she tried, she couldn't remember taking care of the baby or herself. She had fainted, that's why. But his voice. She heard his voice. But what had he said?

"Do not be afraid." That's what he said. Who was he?

"Thank you, Son." Her voice scratched. The baby nuzzled her side.

"Ma, you're awake. The man you were, but you didn't wake up."

"What man?"

"The man who was here. He fixed the fire and said to take care of you. He said Pa was in heaven. He won't come back?"

Belle nodded. Somehow she heard the man's voice again. He had said that. "Did you see him leave?"

Abel knelt beside her. "No." He touched the baby's face. "I have a sister."

"How do you know that?"

"He said so."

"Oh." Such a little word with such a wealth of meaning.

"Merry Christmas, Ma, and Angel, too."

"Angel?"

Abel nodded in his definite four-year-old way. "I named her."

Belle heaved a sigh of relief, of joy, of… She wasn't sure what all, but their Angel was surely a gift of peace. The gift beside her squirmed again and whimpered, going to a full-throated wail on the next breath.

"She's hungry."

"Ja, she is." *Can I get up to sit in the rocker Anson made for me?* Without another thought, she rolled to her knees, babe in her arm, stood, and walked the three feet to the chair and sat. No pain, no weakness. "Please bring me your quilt, Abel."

Setting the baby to nursing was easy, too. Angel latched onto the nipple like she'd done this many times and nursed, her gaze on her mother's face. Belle sucked in a deep breath and let herself relax. *Thank You, dear Father, for the miracles I see all around me: Angel in my arms, and I am sure an angel came to visit us. Thank You for keeping my Anson safe and now home with You.* That the room was warm was miracle enough for right now. The others she would think about later. Now she understood the verse, "And Mary pondered all these things in her heart."

She put her daughter to her shoulder and rubbed her back to hear a loud burp that made Abel giggle.

Abel cocked his head and looked toward the door. "Did you hear him?"

"Who?"

"Rusty, that was Rusty's bark. Ma, Rusty's home."

Belle shook her head. "I'm sorry, Son, but—" She heard it, too. At the same time she realized the quiet. The wind had died.

"Pa!" But Abel shook his head. He said to himself, "Pa is in heaven with Jesus." The bark came again, closer, more insistent.

Abel leaped to his feet and headed for the door.

At that moment, a pounding on the door made him look around at his mother, his eyes rounder than the plates on the shelf.

"Bring me the rifle." She spoke softly and nodded to the gun in the corner. Abel did as she said, and when she had a firm grip on it and had it pointed at the door, she told him. "Go ahead, answer it." *Lord, how can this be? Rusty would not leave Anson. Right, but Anson was gone, the man said so.*

Abel lifted the bar and pulled the door open. A two-foot drift blocked the entry, but a brown-and-white bundle of fur leaped over and through it and threw himself at Abel, whining, whimpering, and yipping. The boy rolled on the floor, giggling and clutching at his best friend.

Belle had one eye on the dog and the other on the man with a flat-brimmed hat who filled the doorway.

"If you can give me a broom, I can sweep this out and close the door. That is if I can come in."

"Are you an angel?"

"Not that I know of. In fact, never been called an angel in all my life."

Belle started to rise, but he waved her back. "Let me get the door closed again, and then we can do the proper introductions." Abel had untangled himself from the dog and fetched the twig broom. He handed it to him.

"I think you are an angel, no matter what you say. My pa went to heaven."

"I know." He shut the door.

"How do you know?" Belle shook her head. Nothing more would ever surprise her. If someday she could ever sort all this out. "Come over and warm up at the fire. And Merry Christmas."

He nodded and removed his hat then unbuttoned his heavy wool coat. Standing in front of the fireplace, he rubbed his hands together in the heat. "This feels mighty fine, ma'am. Thank you."

Abel, one fist locked in Rusty's neck ruff, came over to look up in his face. "How come you talk funny?"

"Abel, that wasn't polite."

"Never mind, Miz Stedman. I got me a story to tell you. Wish it could have a happy endin'."

Belle nodded, one foot setting the rocker in motion. "Anson is gone."

"Yes ma'am. He is. He died when I was tryin' to get him to eat and drink something warm. I came upon his camp. Don't know how he kept that fire goin', sick as he was. Dog was watching over him, probably kept him from freezing to death. He said someone took all his supplies, left him for dead. He burned the boards on the wagon."

"I see." A tear rolled down her cheek and dropped on the blanketed infant. "And the mule?"

"Weren't no mule there. Maybe the robbers took that, too."

"How far away from here?"

"Fifteen miles or so. Guess he got too sick to continue. We'll most likely never know what all happened." He paused to remove his coat. "I wrapped his body in my ground sheet and put him under the wagon frame, blocked as well as I could. To keep the wild animals from him. Didn't find another farm between here and there. Didn't mean any disrespect."

Belle nodded. "I understand. Thank you for doing the best you could. And for being there with him." She closed her eyes for a moment, and when she opened them, she sucked in a deep breath at the same time. "Thank you. We don't have much for dinner, but you are welcome to join us."

"Ma'am, I reckon you don't need to be a-fixin' for me. Let me take care of that. You just tell me where to find things."

"We keep our food in a box in the lean-to." Abel looked up from his talk with Rusty. "I will show you."

"Did I hear a hen cacklin'?"

"We brought the chickens and our cow up to the lean-to 'cause Ma couldn't make it to the barn, and she said I was too little to take care of them."

The disgust in his voice made Belle roll her lips together.

"My pa said I was to take care of Ma and our baby. He didn't know if it was a boy or girl. But we got a girl, and her name is Angel."

"How about I go put my horse in the barn? I brought a sack of oats and one of beans. All the other supplies were gone."

"Anson was bringing our winter supplies back."

"So the wagon was full?"

She nodded. "Most likely."

He huffed a sigh. "Shame, ma'am. That surely is a shame. What will you do?"

"Pa always said God would provide." Abel spoke in all seriousness. "He sent us an angel."

"He sure did." Jeremiah smiled at Belle and indicated the baby.

"No, He sent us a real angel. You tell him, Ma."

"We will save that for another time." She watched the man in front of the fireplace. Perhaps God had sent them three angels. The baby in her arms, the visitor of the night, and the man standing right before her.

CHAPTER 4

Seems to me God got us in a real pickle here, Sanchez." Talking to his horse had become habit since Jeremiah rode alone so many miles. Otherwise he might have gone stark raving crazy. He'd heard that happened to homesteaders on these northern plains. The wind here was indeed something to respect. Opening the barn door required a shovel to move away the drifted snow.

That was one prepared woman, he told himself. Now, where would she or that poor husband of hers have kept the shovel?

"Mr. Jennings! Mr. Jennings!" Abel called as he came dragging the shovel. He was so light, he could walk on the snow, far easier than a man or a horse. Jeremiah scolded himself. The boy shouldn't have come out. He should have done something different. What?

Abel handed him the shovel.

"Thanks for the shovel. Now you'd better get back to the house before you freeze."

Abel gave him a disgusted look. "I shoveled snow before."

Backpedaling, Jeremiah figured he'd better be more observant and less opinionated. "I am sure you did. Are there two shovels?"

"One in the barn."

"Okay, we'll get that out, and you can help me."

The boy's eyes lit up. "Can I pet your horse?"

"His name is Sanchez, and he would like that right well." Jeremiah dug out the door enough to swing it open to let his horse in. He didn't need to clear it all. From the looks of the lowering sky, more snow was on its way. "Why don't you run back to the house and ask your ma ..." What did he need? "Uh, if we need more hay up there."

"It's about gone. I fed the cow this morning."

"You want to lead Sanchez inside for me?"

"Ja, sure. You betcha. My pa used to say that." He took the reins and eased the horse around the half-open door.

He could hear Abel talking to his horse in the far stall of the three. A pile of hay filled the remainder of the barn. The other shovel hung on pegs Anson had driven into the sod wall.

Abel was struggling with the cinch strap when Jeremiah reached the stall.

"Here, let me help you." He loosened it, and Abel finished the job. Sanchez turned his head and nuzzled the boy's shoulder.

"He likes me."

Thank you, Sanchez. "He does. You petted him, and he sure does love to be petted." He threw the saddle over the half wall between stalls and stripped off the bridle.

"We melt snow on the stove for the animals to drink."

"You have a bin we can pour the oats in? Hate for the mice to eat it."

"We could take that to the house."

Talking to this child was about as good as talkin' to a man. Did his ma and pa realize how smart he was?

"Do the chickens and cow stay up there all winter?"

"No, first winter we had the lean-to. Pa and Ma built it during the summer."

"I see. You want to fork some hay in here?"

"Ja, I will."

When they finished taking care of the horse, Jeremiah asked if they had a sled to pull hay up to the house.

"I'll get it." The boy scampered out the door and returned, dragging the sled behind him. By the time they had it loaded and pulled to the house, dusk was already falling. Jeremiah parked the sled at the door to the lean-to, and together they forked it in. The chickens clucked as they settled on their roost across the far corner, and the cow rumbled deep in her throat—the comfortable sounds of contented animals. The baby whimpered in the other room, and the mother comforted her. More sounds that spelled home.

Jeremiah sucked in a deep breath. Sounds he had not heard for years immediately brought back a landslide of memories. He could picture his mother rocking the cradle of the newest addition to the family. Ten children had taken up her life. Jeremiah was the eldest and helped when he could. He and his pa and the others, as they grew old enough, planted the cotton, hoed it, and finally—when, thanks to God, there were no natural catastrophes—picked it. After hauling it to the gin, they had some money to buy more seed and even put food on the table. They grew most of their food themselves, with the smaller children helping the most there. He had left home when the others were old enough to take his place. Sharecropping was not the way he wanted to spend his life, so he headed west.

I hope they had a real Christmas this year. Not sure if he meant that as a prayer or ... or what? *You decide, Lord, and thanks.*

And you haven't even written to them for how long? He tried to ignore the voice, but this was Christmas. He should have, he should have, he should have ....

In the main room, Mrs. Stedman was nursing her baby. He figured he should give her some privacy, hard to do in such small spaces. Yet whole families—even two families—lived in spaces like this for years. It made the house he grew up in look huge in his memory.

Today his memory was more enemy than friend.

"Mr. Jennings?" Abel opened the door and stuck his head out. "We can eat now."

Abel and his mother were already at the table with an empty chair waiting. The chair that would always be empty. How was she managing so serenely? After all, this was Christmas. He'd expect she would be dissolving into tears whenever the thoughts of her husband returned.

"Would you please say grace, Mr. Jennings?"

He bowed his head. How long it had been since he had said grace at a table with a woman and child present. "Dear Lord, we thank Thee for food and shelter and new life, and for Thy Son who saved us. Amen."

They joined in his *amen.* He looked up to see a smile so beautiful it made him catch his breath. She might as well be wearing a halo and be dressed in pure white. He swallowed and blinked and was able to breathe again. What had he seen?

"Are you all right, Mr. Jennings?"

"Yes, I am much more than all right. Thank you. And thank you for sharing your meal with me."

"A blessed Christmas, Mr. Jennings." The baby in the cradle beside her chair squeaked, for certain not a cry but—

"Please pass the corn cakes, but help yourself first."

He did as she asked and felt his ears get red. What was the matter with him, daydreaming—if that's what he could call it—like this? Even all those nights just him and Sanchez, his mind had not turned on him like this.

"Is everything all right, Mr. Jennings?"

"Thank you, ma'am. It will be." *What will you live on with no supplies this winter? Do you have enough wood or peat for the stoves?* He'd not seen an overly large wood pile anywhere outside. But then, surely the mister had left them with wood. But out here on the prairie, there was most certainly a lack of trees. What did the farmers burn?

"Would you care for more?"

"No thank you. I had plenty." He thought a moment. "I have some jerky and hard tack in my saddlebags. Would that help?"

"We can't use up your supplies. Thankfully, you already brought us that bag of beans. That will be a big help."

"Did your husband hunt? Surely there is game around here."

"He planned on that, but the weather has been so miserable even the animals went into hiding."

"We saw some…" Abel screwed up his face. "Four or two deer down by the river. They drink there, but now the river is solid frozen."

"Are there rabbits?"

"In the spring."

"Pa said they turn white in the winter so we can't see them."

"I see. Perhaps I could get you a deer?"

"That would be wonderful, but I hate to keep you from your destination. You already helped Anson."

"Not enough, I'm afraid."

Rusty yipped at the door, and Abel went to let him out. "Ma, come see."

Belle rose. "Excuse me."

Jeremiah pushed back his chair. "Wait. There might be…." But no one listened to him. Strange, she had met him with a gun and now went outside without even checking for strangers. Another strange thing to ponder about this place and situation. She drew her shawl around her shoulders and stepped outside with her son. Jeremiah got to the door as she sighed an ooh of pure delight. He stepped out and looked up where they pointed. The aurora borealis danced in every color of the rainbow against the cobalt sky, arcing and spearing to music no one heard but everyone always felt.

"I've never seen it so bright." She turned to Jeremiah, her hand on her son's shoulder. "Only the Lord could create such glory that it stops your breath."

The cold is what is stopping your breath. "Please go back in the house before you freeze out here."

They all rushed to the fireplace and warmed themselves.

"I'll be saying good night then," Jeremiah said when Abel started to yawn. "Do you mind if I sleep in the barn?"

"That would be fine, but perhaps you would like to sleep in the lean-to tonight? Up against the chimney would be warmer than the barn."

"Thank you. I will do that."

"Do you have enough bedding?"

"I have my bedroll." He rose and reached for his coat. "I'll go on out to the barn and get it." Hat in place, he tipped his head. "Thank you for welcoming me into your home." As he stepped into the night, he heard her say, "Lord bless your sleep, Mr. Jennings."

He stared up at the sky so deep blue as to be almost black with pinpoint stars tacking it in place. "You coulda done better by her, Lord. How on earth is she going to make it through the winter?"

CHAPTER 5

Good morning, Mr. Jennings. I'm sorry we have no real coffee, but I have some oats roasting, and that makes an adequate morning drink." She motioned to a pan over the fireplace fire.

"That smells good enough to eat."

"I know." She checked the sleeping baby under the blanket against her shoulder and lowered her gently into the cradle.

"Your rooster sure likes getting up early. Near to lifted me right out of bed."

"Yes, he figures getting the sun going is all up to him." Her smile made it real easy to return one.

He caught a yawn behind his hand and stretched his neck. "That cow looks like she'll be calving today,"

"Oh, I hope Abel can watch. The last calf was born out in the barn, and he was sad he missed it."

Jeremiah warmed his hands over the stove where snow was melting in the pot. "Did you never sleep?"

"Oh yes, but when a baby wants to eat every two hours or so … I've been up for a while. I don't mind—she is such a miracle." She stretched and crossed to the fire to use her apron to remove the dutch oven from the fire.

"Now I can use some of that water to make the coffee. In a couple of days, we'll have cream for the coffee again." As she talked, she poured water over the oats and put them back over the fire.

"Breakfast will be ready soon. Cornmeal mush, but at least it will be hot and filling."

He laid a once-white bag on the table. "Put some of that jerky in with the beans for flavor. I'm going to see if I can find rabbit or deer trails out there."

"Eat first."

"Ma, is Pa coming today?"

She watched her son's face collapse upon itself as awareness hit him.

"I want Pa to come back." Tears leaked down his cheeks, but he dashed them away.

She held out her arms, and he ran to them. Hugging him close, she smoothed his hair down and laid her cheek on his head, crooning softly all the while. She guided him over to the rocker and sat, lifting him to her lap. They rocked, and when she glanced up, Mr. Jennings was closing the door behind him. At her knee, Rusty looked toward the door and snuggled up as close to his boy as he was able, his quivering body doing everything he could to comfort.

Abel laid his hand on the dog's head. He sniffed and knuckle-rubbed his eyes. "He is with Jesus." His matter-of-fact tone said the tears were done for now. He slid to the floor and reached up to pat his mother's cheek. "I will feed the chickens."

"Mr. Jennings said Tulip might have her calf today."

"Good." He returned to the rope-strung bed he shared with his mother and pulled on his clothes. "Need more snow?"

Belle watched her son. Not yet five and so grown up. When his pa said he was to take care of her, Abel seemed to have left childhood behind and stepped into the role of a small man. How sad. How necessary. If she allowed her mind to go screaming forward, she would start to shake again. Instead, she did what her mother had taught her: thank God for what she had, for all His blessings, and rest in His mighty arms so He could take care of her. And He would. That baby sleeping in the cradle was proof of His mercy.

Abel finished tying his boots, stood, and stamped his feet. With a sniff he shrugged into his coat and stepped out into the lean-to.

Anson always did that. The thought sent an arrow straight through her heart. Sniffing back tears, she raised her chin. Abel did not need to see his mother dissolve into a puddle of tears. She'd cried plenty of them in the middle of the night when Angel let her know it was time to eat. That was when she'd comforted herself with the same words she gave her son. *Someday, Anson, I will see you again.*

But in the meantime … Angel started fussing in earnest. Saved by a baby's needs. Putting the light blanket over her shoulder, she set the round-faced baby to her breast and the rocker to creaking. In the quiet of the night, the rocker song had spoken to her of Anson's care for her and his family. He'd crafted this chair as a gift, a tangible proof of his caring that would stay with her. But he never had said he loved her.

She made the coffee, and she and Abel ate the mush. They poured the hot water over more snow to water the chickens and offered some to the cow, but she turned her head. It looked like their guest had shoveled the manure out the door. With the packed-dirt floor, it was relatively easy to clean up after the cow and the chickens.

After setting beans to cooking, adding small pieces of jerky, and moving the pot back to simmer, she swept the floor and brought in more snow to melt.

"A rifle shot!" Abel leaped up from playing with bits of wood on the floor in front of the fireplace. Together they ran to the frond-frosted window and blew on the glass enough to peek out, only to see snow and more snow. Footprints led toward the river. She motioned to Abel, and they stuck their heads out the door. Rusty pushed past them and headed out across the snow, his feet throwing up miniature snow clouds. She started to turn away when she saw a brown, flat-brimmed hat rising from the riverbank. As the man appeared, she realized he was dragging something. Something brown and, from the looks of it, very heavy.

"A deer. He shot a deer." Visions of chops frying and a haunch roasting over the fire floated through her mind. She could smell the fragrance and hear it sizzling. *Thank You, Lord.* Food to make it through at least the worst of the winter, especially if she hoarded it like a miser did gold.

Rusty darted back and forth, barking at the carcass, then danced around Mr. Jennings, yipping delight and throwing snow everywhere. True, even the dog would enjoy the spoils. "Oh Lord, thank You for providing again." Although she knew how to shoot a gun—Anson had made sure of that—she'd never shot at anything. Or killed something other than chickens. But she knew that if she had to learn to hunt, she would do that. With their nearest neighbor several miles away, the visits were few and far between. The homestead between this one and the other had been abandoned when the summer sun burned out the wheat crop. The oat harvest had been meager.

But she had hauled water from the river to water their garden enough to get at least some food that lasted through early December. After Anson left for supplies. She should have hoarded the vegetables more wisely.

"Come on, Ma, come see." Abel beckoned her from the door. He had gone outside shortly after he heard the shot.

Belle wrapped her shawl over her head and pulled on her winter coat. Stepping outside, she wished for a hat brim. Amazing how it could be storming one day or even one hour, and the next the sun blinded your eyes, reflecting off the sparkling snow.

"He was too heavy to carry," Mr. Jennings called. "I'll take the carcass to the barn. Did your husband set up a pulley system there for hanging game?"

"He did. You'll find the rope tied to a stall post. He carved the pulley himself."

"This should feed you for much of the winter." He stopped, his breath blowing clouds of steam around his face. His smile caught at her heart. What a shame he didn't use it more often. Anson had a smile, too, that had not had enough exercise. She wasn't surprised. This land stole smiles from lots of faces.

"You can fry the liver for dinner. And the heart could bake real well in that dutch oven in the fireplace. Come on, Abel, you can help me." He tipped his hat to Belle. "He can bring the liver up while I skin the rest."

"What a gift. Thank you, Mr. Jennings."

Some minutes later, Abel brought a bucket up with the heart and liver and grunted as he lifted the bucket up on the table. "Mr. Jennings said I am a good helper."

"He's right. You most certainly are. I think I heard a hen cackle when I was feeding Angel. You want to check for eggs, too?"

"Ma, come quick!" He motioned for her to hurry.

"Now what?"

"Tulip—she's falling apart."

Belle dipped her hands in a bucket of water heating on the stove and, drying them on her apron, joined him in the lean-to. Tulip lay on her side with two small hooves showing. She moaned, and the ankles appeared as the contraction did its job.

"That's the calf. Stay back. Now the legs, and see the nose is coming on top of the legs." *Oh you poor girl, I know just what you feel like.* "Come on, Tulip, push some more."

Abel looked up at his mother, eyes round as his mouth. "The calf is inside her."

"Yes." She steeled herself for his next question. Sure as that calf would soon be here, her son stared from her to the cow and back at her middle.

"Was Angel inside you?"

"Yes."

The cow moaned again and gave a mighty push, and the calf slithered out onto the hay scattered on the floor.

"Ooh, look." He started forward, but she stopped him with her hands on his shoulders. "You stay back in case she starts to move around." Belle bent over by the calf and, using a wisp of hay, cleared the mucus from the baby's nose. The cow lurched to her feet and started cleaning her now-alert baby up.

"Good girl," murmured Belle, looking around to see if there was anything to help dry the calf. "Go get one of those rags behind the stove."

Abel returned quickly and handed it to his mother. "Can I pet it? Is it a boy or a girl?"

He stepped forward, and the cow raised her head, glaring at him. "How come she doesn't like me anymore?"

"Because she has a calf and knows it is her job to protect her baby. And I don't know yet if it's a boy or girl."

The calf shook its head. The cow made noises deep in her throat and kept licking her baby. Within a few minutes, the calf tried straightening its legs. Rump in the air, it tried to do the same with the front legs but toppled back to the ground. On the third try, it stood.

"We have a male calf, a little bull."

"Like me."

Belle rolled her lips together and nodded, standing back to watch the little guy find his mother's udder and latch on to a teat.

"He's eating." Abel looked up to his mother, a grin splitting his face. "Tulip is a good mother."

"Ja, she is."

"Well, look at that." Jeremiah stopped in the doorway from the kitchen. "Looks to be a right smart calf there. What will you name it?"

Belle smiled down at her son. "You choose."

"I have to think about it. Can we eat now? I'm hungry."

"As soon as I fry the liver. Sorry, Mr. Jennings, we got a bit sidetracked here."

"The deer is hanging. I do hope it doesn't freeze tonight. We might want to hang it in here. Plenty cold but not freezing."

"Whatever you think best. I'm just thankful we have meat." Meat and beans and cornmeal, with milk soon. What a Christmas season this was turning into.

CHAPTER 6

I'm sorry, Reverend Swenson," Belle said to her pastor, who had arrived just as she was getting ready to cook up the liver. "I just cannot put someone out like that. Not unless it is absolutely necessary. I know my neighbors. They don't have any more than we have. And besides, Anson and I agreed if something happened to one of us, the other would stay right here."

Of course she didn't tell him that they never figured the mule would not be here and that one of them really would die. So soon at least. Although the fear of dying in childbirth had not really left until the angel came. Somehow, ever since that, she'd not been afraid of anything, not the wind and the wolves that howled, not being alone.

Had she really heard him say, "Do not be afraid"? Or? Or what? She most certainly had more questions than answers.

"Good of you to come check on us like this. I appreciate it."

"You are indeed welcome."

But what if Jeremiah leaves?

When had she started to think of him as Jeremiah? It wasn't like he had been here long, but somehow it seemed like half a lifetime.

"Well, the way that wind is picking up, I'd better be on my way. You know my wife will nail my hide to the cabin wall when I come back and tell her all this and you are not with me?"

"I'm sorry to hear that. You'll definitely do better with your hide in place."

He had the grace to smile at her attempt at humor. He stood and set his cup on the table.

"I'll get the heart for you." She headed out to the lean-to and the box they stored food in where she had set the heart and liver for protection. Tulip watched her, the calf peeking around his mother's dewlap. "I'm not going to bother you now, but tonight I will be milking you, so you better be prepared."

She wrapped the meat in a cloth with its ends tied together to make a sack of sorts and took it back to the reverend. "Tell the missus it weren't your fault You gave it your best, but as Anson always said, 'Claribelle Stedman was just another name for stubborn.' "

She showed him to the door with a smile. The wind tried to grab the door, but she held tight. "You sure you should go out in this?"

"Not snowing yet, but that old horse of mine would find his way back to the feed box in a blizzard in the middle of the night." He tucked his scarf in around his neck and over the lower part of his face. "Fact is, he has. The good Lord makes sure I get where I need to go."

He mounted and rode off the way he came.

Belle shut the door and dropped the bar in place. The storm wasn't really on them yet—if it did indeed attack like the others had. Sometimes they just blew on by. Weather could be downright capricious.

She looked up to see Jeremiah shaking his head. "I can take you somewhere else soon as the weather lets up. You know that."

"I know, but I will tell you the same. I am staying here."

"What's so all-fired important about this piece of land that you won't leave even for a time?" He tried to keep the impatience out of his voice. After all, this was none of his business really, but the look she gave him let him know she got the point.

"I know you can't see it through the snow, but all our blood, sweat, and tears for four years watered this land. Anson has died for this land."

"Well, not exactly." He started to say something else and thought the better of it. "Think I'll go milk Tulip."

"Don't throw the colostrum away. The calf can drink it later, and the chickens will like it."

"My ma used to say colostrum was good for whatever ailed you."

"I'll make a pudding, and we even have sugar to put in it, thanks to Reverend Swenson. Oh such a treat this will be." She almost sang. She spun around. "We could even put a dollop of jam on top. Something lovely." She glanced at Jeremiah, to see him staring at her, a half smile in place, slightly shaking his head. "What?"

"Who were you before you married Anson and moved to the frontier?"

"This isn't exactly a frontier, you know. Why Dakota Territory might become a state sometime soon."

"Be that as it may..." He raised an eyebrow, along with a bucket, used and scrubbed so much it almost shone inside. "Use this for milking?"

"Yes. If it is big enough. I can make cheese, too. Ma used to make good cheese from the early milk." A cloud tried to darken the sunshine. "Before." She sucked in a breath and smiled down at her son. "Pretty soon you will have to learn to milk, too. If your hands are strong enough."

"Pa said I am strong."

"Ma said it, too."

He nodded. "Will the calf mind?"

"He might mind, but it will do no good. He will have to learn to drink from a bucket or Tulip won't keep producing enough milk for all of us."

"Why not?"

"Because the calf can't drink as much milk as Tulip can make."

"Oh." His brow wrinkled as he nodded. Then he looked up at his mother with a sun-kissed grin. "But we can."

"We can. We will have butter and cheese and cream in our coffee and buttermilk for us and the chickens and—"

Angel announced her displeasure at being ignored.

Belle blew up a breath from her lower lip that lifted the wisps of hair framing her face. And Anson wasn't there to enjoy this with them. The cloud tried to descend again. But Jeremiah was. He would like the pudding. And the cheese. If he stayed. He said he had to leave.

But I don't want him to leave. Where had that thought come from? Of course she didn't want him to leave in the middle of the storm, danger, all the things that were sure to assail him on his way north and west. She would be concerned for anyone going out in this.

So why did you not protest when Reverend Swenson left? Now that was a silly question. He had a home not more than three or four miles away, while Jeremiah was not exactly sure even where he was going. Well, he had a map, but he'd not been there before. Like when she and Anson came to the stakes he had set out when he filed his homestead papers.

She picked up Angel, and they nestled into the chair. Feeding her baby was one of the most pleasurable things she had ever done, even though it got a bit uncomfortable at times. But she remembered from nursing Abel that the discomfort went away—a small price to pay for the joy of a baby. With her toe, she pushed just enough to rock gently. Angel nursed like she'd not been fed for two days. Already she waved her tiny fist. Belle didn't remember Abel doing that until he was weeks or more old. Angel did not act like a three-day-old baby, that was for sure.

She could hear Abel talking to Jeremiah out in the lean-to. Peace filled the room and her heart. What if Jeremiah would stay?

He couldn't stay here; that wasn't proper. What few neighbors she had would be terribly offended, first that someone beside Anson was living here, and second that she'd not honored the year-long decree of mourning behavior for a widow. *Lord God, I don't even own a black dress.* A dark blue one but not black. Anson used to make remarks about the strictures of society. He'd wanted no part of that.

But he was gone. That was the final line. Had she loved him? He had never said he loved her. Being a man of few words meant not wasting any. Was telling your wife that you loved her a waste of words?

Lord, why am I thinking all these outrageous thoughts now? I've never thought them before. Where did they come from?

"Ma!" Abel burst through the door. "The calf sucked on my fingers!" He held up his hand. "He liked them."

"Why?"

"'Cause I put my fingers into the milk like Mr. Jennings said." He wiggled his fingers and giggled.

Little boy laughter was entirely contagious, so she smiled back and then laughed, too. Laughter was a much-needed commodity in this household. Life was too serious. And death even more so. But today they could laugh. Was that a gift from the angel, too?

CHAPTER 7

That was really good," Jeremiah said as he leaned back in his chair after their delayed meal of fried liver.

"Thank you. I'm glad you liked it." Belle glanced over to the cradle where her daughter was making noises.

"Angel's crying," Abel said as if his mother should answer immediately.

"Thank you, but she's just waking up."

Angel took that moment to break into a wail.

Abel looked at his mother and shook his head, just the tiniest amount.

Belle stared at her son. "She wasn't really crying, you know."

His eyebrows twitched.

Belle rose and picked up her infant from the cradle, snuggling the baby against her shoulder. Angel calmed long enough to be laid down, but when Belle removed her diaper, she started in again. "Sh, sh, little one. I'm hurrying." Bundling her back up, she sat down in the rocker and, blanket over her shoulder, positioned the baby for nursing.

Jeremiah almost laughed at the byplay between mother and son. What made the boy so conscious of the baby? Was it because he'd never had a baby around before? He rose and gathered the dishes together, setting them in the pan of soapy water steaming on the stove.

"You don't have to do that," she said.

"I know. Abel and I are goin' to the barn this afternoon to check on that deer. Maybe bringing it up to the lean-to so it won't freeze, but the smell of blood might upset the new mother out there."

"Would it be terrible if the deer froze?"

"Need to cut it up first, and it should hang at least a day before we do that."

"I see."

She looked so peaceful he wanted to just sit and watch, but that wouldn't be polite, least ways the way he understood proper behavior. Not that handling cattle and living with other cowboys reminded one of polite behavior. But his mother had done her best to instill some sense of propriety in her family in spite of the sparseness of their lives.

So he pushed himself to his feet and, retrieving his coat while Abel did the same, stepped out into the lean-to. "We need to build some kind of a pen for that little varmint there so he can be shut away as his mother's real milk comes in."

"The white kind?"

"Right."

"But why can't he nurse anyway?"

"Cows, like other animals, have a way of making enough milk for their own baby, and we want her to make enough milk for your family. So if we pen the calf, she will keep producing more."

Abel stared at the cow, then up at the man. "How does she know all that? Who told her?"

"That's one of God's secrets, I guess."

"He can talk cow, too?"

The desire to laugh out loud felt so good, but instead Jeremiah nodded and smiled. "God can talk any kind of language He wants."

"Dog, too?"

"Dog, too." Jeremiah handed him the carved wooden pitchfork. "You want to clean out the manure? We'll put it by the house for now—helps keep the house warmer—but later it goes out in the garden. You do have a garden, right?"

Abel nodded and almost jabbed Jeremiah with the end of the pitchfork since the space was so crowded. "We got to fill the buckets with snow, too."

So many things he'd not had to do in Texas. While it snowed there a few times, it never stayed around long enough for more than a passing acquaintance. Not like this, where the snow took up residence for months on end. What would this country look like, all greened up for spring? Was the ranch he was heading for like this, or would it be more like Texas?

The urge to get on the trail again caught him by surprise. He'd given his word, and as far as Mr. Stubb knew, he was already there. He'd thought he heard the lonesome whistle of a train weeping out across the snowdrifted prairie. If he had any money, he'd have taken the train, but they'd been told it didn't go north and south yet, so what good would it do? The map he'd studied before leaving didn't begin to show him how far the ranch really was.

"You know if there are any boards out in the barn?"

"Some poles Pa brought back from the river one day."

"That'll work. Come on, you can show me."

By the time they had cut and pounded two rails into the sod wall across the corner and attached them to a movable post, dusk had blued the snowbanks. They watered the cow and horse and refilled all the buckets to melt again.

A small tub steamed on the stove.

"What you making, Ma?"

"Your baby sister needs clean diapers."

"You cook them?" He stared at her, making both adults chuckle.

"Don't worry, I made real food for us. We can eat as soon as you are ready."

Abel shook his head and glanced down at the cradle. "Babies are a lot of work."

Jeremiah laid a hand on the boy's shoulder. "Come on, let's get Tulip milked, and you can feed the calf. What are you goin' to name him?" They stepped back out into the nearly dark lean-to.

Abel shook his head. "I don't know." He stopped. "What about Nosey? He's always nosing for more to eat."

"Nosey it is."

The jerky-flavored beans made for a good meal. But that night in his bedroll, Jeremiah's mind would not shut down no matter how tired his body was. The realization was heavy with no easy answers. How would he ever be able to leave this woman and her children alone out here on the prairie with no near neighbors and not even a mule to go for help if needed? Yet he had given his word to take over the northern spread. *Dear Lord, what am I to do?*

CHAPTER 8

The next morning, Jeremiah couldn't decide whether the snow was still coming down or only blowing up from the earlier snowfall. Today was the day he absolutely should leave. But first he had to cut up that deer. If he quartered it, Belle could at least handle the sections, but even that would not be easy. Did she have a smokehouse? A box to let it freeze in? What should he do with the hide? Did she know how to tan a hide? So many questions and no easy answers.

He folded up his bedroll once he heard her in the kitchen. Now he could get a bucket to milk the cow again. After making pudding, Belle had set a pot of the colostrum to heating by the fire to make cheese. Once it turned to curd, she'd hang it to drain, and she said she'd start another pot. She was so thrilled to have the colostrum, he'd begun to realize she was happy to have anything. Instead of asking for more, she rejoiced over what she had just been given. He knew for certain there was a lesson there for him, too.

How can I leave her?

He kept coming back to that terrible, horrible question. He had to convince her to either get someone else to stay with them out here or go stay with someone else. Someone would make room at their house; that was the way things were done in the West.

"Good morning, Mr. Jennings. I'm sorry if I woke you."

"I was already awake."

"The coffee will be hot soon."

"Thank you." Such a stilted conversation. "How is Angel this morning?"

"She was hungry. That baby eats like none else I have known."

"She seems older than four days."

"Seems that way to me, too." She reached for one of the cups on the shelf and, cup in hand, turned to look at him. "I have to confess something."

"You do?" *Seems upside down to me. I'm the one who needs to confess—not just something, but a whole lot.*

"Yes." She looked down at the cup in her hand. "I feel so guilty that you are missing out on your job because you feel the need to stay here and take care of us. We will be all right. You have to believe that."

Jeremiah tipped his head back to stare at the rafters above. No wonder this house was cold—all the heat went up to the roof. The thought made him shake his head. As if that had anything to do with the fix they were in.

"The only way I can leave you here is if someone else comes to stay or you move into another house until spring comes."

"If I had a horse or mule, then I would be able to ride for help. Surely that would suffice."

"But what if you were the one who was sick? How would Abel, small as he is, go for help?"

"True." She stared into the empty cup.

He watched her face grow stern. When she looked at him, he saw a whole different person staring back at him.

"You are not responsible for me, for us, Jeremiah Jennings. Since Anson has gone to his reward, God and I are responsible for us. You keep your word, and I will keep mine."

He gritted his teeth, the urge to yell at her almost more than he could handle. "I am going to milk the cow. She at least will listen to reason. This can be used to water her, right?"

"Right!"

But he couldn't do it. He lost the inner battle. "You have to have help! You can—not—live—here—by—your—self!" He knew he was shouting, or at least raising his voice. He knew he cut each word with a sword. A sharp sword.

The baby started to cry. Abel woke up, crying and rubbing his eyes. Even the cow mooed and the rooster crowed.

"Why are you yelling at me? You have no—"

"Because I love you!"

You could have heard a feather float.

She paused in the act of lifting the baby and stared at him.

He stared at her.

A pint-sized warrior planted himself in front of Jeremiah. "Why are you yelling at my ma?" How could one small person, too little to mount a horse, pack so much venom into a simple sentence?

His mind screamed, *Run!* His body screamed, *Run!*

But Jeremiah Jennings could not run or turn or—

He took two steps forward, around the warrior with tears streaming down his cheeks and his fists planted firmly on his skinny hips, and three more steps to do a military halt in front of the woman who could never be his enemy and right now didn't believe he was a friend.

"Marry me!"

Tears erupted. "No one has ever said those words to me—'I love you.' "

"Well, I never said them before either, so that makes us even. But I have never meant anything more in my life. I love you. I love Abel and Angel. And I want to marry all of you. Right now, today."

She closed her eyes, but the tears refused to stop. "I—I can't."

"You can't what? Love me? Marry me? Pour the coffee? You can't what?" He didn't dare touch her, or he knew he would kiss her until they couldn't breathe. So he carefully set the bucket on the floor and glued his hands to his sides. *Lord, I need some real help here, right now!* He sniffed. "Please stop cryin'. I can't bear to see you cry. What can I do?"

"I—I c-can't."

He waited. Leaned forward. "You can't what?" Love me? I'll wait. Marry me? I'll wait. Quit crying? He dug in his pocket and brought out a handkerchief that had surely seen better days. He started to offer that to her but changed his mind. His handkerchief might make her throw up. He leaned over by the stove and snatched a cloth then mopped her cheeks, his touch like that of angel wings.

"Sh-sh-sh. Don't cry. All will be well. Don't cry." His mother always said that—*"All will be well."* He had come to believe every word of it through the years.

He repeated it, more strongly. He looked down to see Abel, fist wrapped in his mother's apron, staring up at him, question marks all over his face.

"It's all right, son. All will be well."

He guided Belle so her legs backed against the chair, and he lowered her into it. He mopped her tears again and smiled when she finally opened her eyes. "All right now?"

She nodded, swallowed, and swallowed again.

Angel whimpered.

Jeremiah sucked in a deep breath and squatted down to eye level with Abel. "Come on. Let's get you dressed before your feet freeze off."

The boy glanced down at his feet and nodded. He stuck his hand into Jeremiah's. "Can I help you milk Tulip?"

Jeremiah tried not to laugh, but the effort rocked him back, butt square on the floor. He didn't just laugh, he guffawed, pulling the boy into his lap, and gathered his little feet into one hand while he circled the child with his other arm. "Yep, you can help me milk Tulip. She'll be telling us to hurry on out there anytime now." He gave Belle a wink. "We'll be talking about this again. You can count on it." He surged to his feet, child in his arms. "You cannot milk a cow in your nightshirt. It just ain't proper."

He turned to smile at Belle. "I'll be back."

After brushing off Tulip's udder, he sat down, put the bucket between his knees, and planted his forehead in her flank. "This is the way you sit when you milk. Then, using two hands, you squeeze and release, pulling down gently at the same time. Like this, see?" The milk began squirting into the bucket. Once he'd milked so the bottom of the bucket was covered, he motioned Abel to come beside him. "Now you lean in here and put your hand on one teat, and I'll put my hand over yours." When the milk again squirted into the bucket, now foaming, Abel giggled.

"Feels warm and funny."

"That it does. Okay, tomorrow you can sit on the stool and try it. You pretend with me now. Right hand, left hand." The milk music picked up again. Nosey bawled from the pen where he now lived. "Right hand, left hand."

"Milking is hard work."

"Not so much after your arms and hands get used to it." When he'd finished, he stood and hung the stool back up on the peg on the wall. "Now you feed Nosey." He poured milk into another bucket.

Abel held the bucket in place and stuck his fingers down in the milk, and when Nosey remembered what he was supposed to do, he found his fingers and sucked away.

"Tonight you take your fingers away and see if he will do it alone."

Abel nodded and, when the bucket was empty, carried it into the house. "I did it. I sorta milked, and I fed Nosey. He likes my fingers." He looked down his arm and frowned. "I got my sleeve wet."

"Milk will wash out. I'm proud of you."

"When I can milk, you won't have to."

"That's right."

Jeremiah poured the milk through a towel into a kettle. "You want this by the fire, too?"

"Yes, please. The mush is ready."

Abel went to the window. "The sun is shining."

"I know. You need to bring in some wood."

While he did that, Jeremiah looked at Belle. "We need to talk."

She nodded. "That we do."

At least she looked more agreeable, he thought, puffing a sigh. "I'll sharpen the knives to cut the meat, and then we can let it freeze outside tonight. Tonight we'll talk."

She didn't smile when she nodded.

Maybe he didn't really want to talk, he thought. He might not like her answers.

CHAPTER 9

We have to talk. Jeremiah had talked too much already, way too much. Love her? He respected her, was proud of her, liked her and her fiery stubbornness. But love? He didn't even know what love was, not really. His mother bore his father ten kids, but did she love him? She called him *that hateful man* on more than one occasion. She got angry at him.

And Jeremiah was angry with this Belle Stedman right now. Her stubbornness endangered herself and her children. Endangered her man-cub Abel and her helpless baby. Maybe she didn't have any love. But no, that was foolish thinking. He thought about her gentle touch, the way she spoke to Abel, the way she cuddled her tiny girl. No, she was full of love. Just not for him.

He tossed Sanchez some hay and rubbed the nose of his easygoing old roan. But the horse was more interested in the hay than in his master just now. He dropped his grizzled head to the ground and began munching and crunching supper.

The last traces of sun were entirely gone, inside the barn and out. Jeremiah groped his way through the darkness down the rough-hewn stanchions to the door and stepped outside, closing the door behind him. There they were back again, the auroras, the mysterious, shimmering curtains moving among the stars.

Did anyone have any idea how or why those things appeared? They did not occur in Texas. That was for sure. Did the snow and the piercing cold play a part?

Who cared, really? There they were. *Ignore 'em, admire 'em, but just don't pick 'em apart.*

The path along the rope strung from the barn to the house had been packed down solid. It was part level track, part ice. He stomped the snow off his boots, rapped on the door, and entered.

Abel stirred on his pallet, but he was asleep. Belle was nearly asleep. Wrapped in a heavy woolen shawl, she rocked slowly, dreamily beside the woodstove with her baby on her lap.

She opened her eyes. She smiled then, and his whole world lit up.

He grabbed a stool from the table and plunked it down beside her rocker so he could sit on it facing her, his shoulder by her knee. The stove and its welcome heat was right in front of him. "I been thinking a good bit about what popped out of me earlier. Loving you." He didn't know how to say what he really thought. He'd never had to before, especially not to a woman. "Been thinking—maybe it isn't love. But if not, it's awful close."

She studied him. She didn't stare, didn't look surprised or angry or anything else. Thoughtful, if anything. He wasn't good at reading women's faces, but hers was about as easy to read as anyone's. She took a long, deep breath. "Are you married?"

"No. Never have been." He smiled. "Left home as soon as I could and grew up on a Texas ranch. You know how you have neighbors you can walk to? You don't walk to the neighbors in Texas; the spreads are scattered too far apart. And no women."

"You seem comfortable with Abel. The baby, too."

"Nine little brothers and sisters. I've changed a diaper before." The smile faded. "That's part of why I said that today, I think, about loving and marrying. I like kids. I like yours, a lot."

"You understand about homestead law?"

"Not really."

She licked her lips. "We laid a homestead claim on this property and marked it off. We developed it—that is, built a house and barns and fences and planted fields and gardens. Ran livestock of some sort. The cow counts as livestock, and the chickens. We used to have a pig, but we ate it. In short, we met the law by settling onto our claim like we're going to stay. If we stay on the land for five years and farm it, we prove it up. That means we gain title to it. If we leave the land, we have to start over somewhere else. That's the Homestead Act."

"How long have you been here?"

"This is starting into the fifth year. This land is nearly ours." Her voice broke. "Mine." She took another deep breath. Her voice went solid again. "You feel a need to go to your boss's other ranch."

"More than need. A responsibility."

She nodded. "If I were to go with you, I would be abandoning this land before it's proved up. Therefore I would lose it. This land is my children's future. Their legacy. Their father worked hard to provide this for them, and so did I. I can't leave it."

"So it's not just stubbornness." He nodded. He dropped forward to prop his elbows on his knees and stare at the floor awhile. Not floor. Rug. The floor was beaten earth, but she'd made some sort of braided rug to cover most of it. And that rug—how long had it taken to braid a rug this big out of wool scraps? The rug sort of said what she was saying—an untold lot of work had gone into this place to make it a home. A home forever. And he understood.

"Why is it such a responsibility? I thought a boss was someone you worked for, got your pay, and if you decided to work somewhere else, you quit and took the other job."

He smiled again. "That's how it usually works, yeah. But not this time. You see, I was sort of flounderin'. Seventeen years old, never worked at anything except sharecroppin'. Helpin' Pa in the fields. And helpin' Ma with the little brothers and sisters. Soon as Ellie Mae and Annie Mae were old enough to take care of the kids, I left. Pa was hoppin' mad. With sharecroppin', the more kids you have, the more money you can make. I promised to send money home, but I almost never did; I didn't make enough money to send anywhere. Then Mr. Stubb sort of took me under his wing."

"Mr. Stubb was your boss?"

The baby gurgled and stretched then began to fuss. Belle lifted her to her shoulder and rubbed her back.

Jeremiah nodded. "I came to his ranch looking for a job. No money, not a penny. Just a hungry, scrawny, grumpy kid. He fed me and hired me; took me in, really. He and the missus taught me manners, taught me ciphering, taught me about our Savior. Workin' in the fields back home, I never would've learnt any of that."

"So you owe him everything, even your eternal life."

She did understand. What a woman! He bobbed his head. "Exactly."

"Your father was a hard man."

"Still is. I guess. Haven't wrote home for a long time; don't know if he's livin' or dead." He looked at her. "What about you? What's your story?"

She didn't answer right away, as if she was thinking about it. Then she said, "It is incredibly difficult, maybe even impossible, for one person, man or woman, to prove up on a homestead. There's just too much to do. Too much work. But it's a way to own land, a farm, when you don't have any money. My father worked for the railroad, but only three days a week. Anson's father lost his job as a telegraph operator. Heavy drinking. So neither Anson nor I had any money. We knew each other from going to the same school. When we graduated from eighth grade."

"Where?"

"Missouri. Independence. Anson said, 'We can be farmers and landowners with this Homestead Act. Let's do it. Let's marry and do it.' So we married, claimed here near the railroad, and … well, that was the dream."

"Didn't you love him at all?"

"Oh, I liked him all right. He was a masterful craftsman. Look at this rocker. Graceful looking, but solid as a rock. And the house. He built the whole house; I only helped a little because I was busy with the garden and chickens, and then with Abel." She studied the rug, too. "And he was very good at accepting responsibility. He chose to be a family man, so he took care of his family. That has to be something to love."

"Love? Or respect?"

She smiled and sniffed and nodded. "*Respect* is a much better word. Yes, I respected him and all his hard work. It must not be lost."

His mind whirled as did his heart. He didn't like any of this. "So the best I can see, we're doomed."

"Doomed?"

"I gotta go to Mr. Stubb's ranch; you gotta stay here. I can't let you stay here alone, but I can't do anything else." He shrugged. "We're doomed." And then he asked what he was terribly afraid to ask but had to ask anyway. "Do you love me?"

She thought a moment. He admired that in her: not just saying whatever jumped into her head, like he did so often. "I don't know for sure. I don't know if I ever really felt love. I think I do." She smiled sadly. "But like you say, we're doomed."

CHAPTER 10

Jeremiah liked that Reverend Swenson fellow; he was a man of his word. Here he came up the track, driving a sleigh with two men on horseback at his side. Jeremiah laid aside the rail with which he was repairing the barn-side corral and walked out to meet them.

The reverend drove into the yard. "Mr. Jennings. Good morning."

Rusty came bounding over, tail flailing, and barked a greeting to his friends.

"Mornin', Reverend. Not quite sure about all this. Are you a pastor or a minister or a rector or a vicar?"

Reverend Swenson laughed. "A pastor. May I introduce Marcus Smith and Sam Barhold? They're members of our church in town. We've come out to retrieve the body of poor Anson Stedman."

"Ah, of course."

Belle stepped out onto the porch. "Good morning, Reverend! Marcus, Sam. Coffee's made."

The reverend tipped his hat. "We'd like Mr. Jennings here to take us out and show us where, uh, the mortal remains are."

She froze. And then—and this was very curious—Jeremiah could just about read her thoughts. Her heart moved from warm cheer and hospitality to sudden ice and sadness. And that was to be expected. "Of course, Reverend Swenson. Perhaps you all will stop by later."

"We shall indeed."

Jeremiah nodded. "I'll saddle up."

He hurried into the dark barn to his roan and saddled as quickly as possible. About the time his eyes were well adjusted to the gloom, he rode out into the brilliance of sun on snow. "Abel? Will you close the barn door, please?" He joined the party as the little boy darted toward the barn, and they all rode out to the east.

Now was a fine time to think of this, but he should have brought Rusty. The dog knew the way; he was not so certain, and he knew Sanchez didn't give a fig. There were precious few landmarks to guide his way on this vast prairie.

The reverend opened conversation. "Several people in our congregation this year have suffered pneumonia. Two died. Is that what struck down Mr. Stedman?"

"S'pose so, but I'm no doctor. He rattled when he breathed. That's usually pneumonia. But the cold had much to do with it."

The reverend nodded. "I understand that Russia refers to this season as 'General Winter.' The Russian army was no match for Napoleon's legions, but the winter cold was. It decimated the French. They were on the verge of taking Moscow—entered the city in fact—but they had to retreat because of the extreme cold. Most died on the way back to France."

Jeremiah nodded grimly. "I see your point. Same cold as this."

"Pretty much. Ah, Mr. Jennings, but wait until you experience spring and summer here. As close to heaven as earth ever gets. And autumn—crisp, clear, flowing gold. So to get to the beautiful seasons, if you will, we put up with the winter."

"Unless it kills you."

Silence.

Nice move, Jennings. You just cast a pall over the whole conversation.

Then the reverend asked, "You sound like you've come up from the South. The accent."

"I have. Texas. There's a man to whom I owe a great deal, a Mr. Stubb. He owns a ranch to the north and west of here. He asked me to take it over because of some problems there. So I'm on my way to do that."

"I see. And you stumbled upon Anson."

"Exactly so. Saw his campfire away up ahead, thought to warm myself, maybe share a meal."

The reverend nodded. "He was a fine man, a good Christian. And his wife no less."

"I figured that out, yes sir. Somebody did a fine job raisin' the both of 'em."

"Indeed." The reverend seemed thoughtful. "Sometimes, though, there's not much the parents can do if a child is wayward. Sparing the rod, applying the rod, doesn't seem to make much difference."

Jeremiah nodded. "That's so. I have two brothers like that." Where were they, anyway? This party, he meant, not his brothers. He knew where his brothers were: one was in jail and the other in Little Rock. "Can't imagine you with a wayward boy, Reverend."

The man smiled. "Not a boy. A niece. Always in trouble, it seems. Not trouble such as lying or stealing. Pranks. Roughhousing. She's twelve now, and old enough to know better. To at least act like a lady."

"I have a sister like that. You want to find her, start lookin' up in trees. Or in the creek catching crawdads. Not where you usually see a girl, like with a doll. And go, go, go."

"Yes! That is Cordellia, exactly. A sweet child but hardly proper."

He was pretty sure they were still on track, because there was a low rise off to the north that he seemed to remember; had a couple scrawny little trees on it like those. But this broad, broad prairie, barely undulating, looked too much the same. Funny how he could make his way across Texas plains just as flat as this and know exactly where he was, but this land? No.

Wait. Up ahead there. What they call a copse, a little rise with some mesquites on it. No, not mesquites this far north, but trees. Or bushes. Something. He pointed. "Let's head over there."

The reverend turned his sleigh aside.

An odd mound of new-fallen snow sat near the bushes. And the bushes were all cut off, as with a knife. Only the thickest branches, too stout to chop with a knife, stuck out, just as he remembered. He swung down, dropped a rein to ground-tie Sanchez, and started beating aside the mound with his hat. Yep. Here it was. Had to be God guidin' him, because he sure wouldn't have picked this out as the spot otherwise. There was the wagon, what was left that Stedman hadn't burned. Three wheels, the frame, the seat boards still attached. Was there anything left of Anson Stedman?

Under the wagon frame, the snow mounded a bit, and that is where he'd left Stedman. He brushed the snow off the mound at one end. A wool scarf. Jeremiah had wrapped the head in the scarf when he laid him out.

Grimly the reverend moved in beside him. Sam and Marcus pressed in close.

Jeremiah knelt at the mound and used his hand to brush away most of the snow from the scarf, tug it up over the head to reveal the corpse's face. Ghastly. That was the word. A strange bluish-white cast to the skin and frozen pure rock solid. His stomach flipped.

The reverend knelt and held a hand over the frozen face, muttering something. Then he said aloud, "I'm glad animals didn't get to him. I suppose that once the remains are frozen, they don't have much scent to attract varmints."

Sam nodded. "'Bout how it is with cattle. I've looked down on many a frozen cow and calf, but it was never like this."

"Amen," said Marcus, and he turned away and threw up.

Jeremiah stood up and tried to move the wagon frame, give them more working room, but it was frozen fast in the old snow.

Wouldn't budge. So the four of them tugged and yanked and managed to get the body rolled out into the open.

Sam wrapped the scarf back around Mr. Stedman's face. Each on a corner, they toted him over to the sleigh and slid him in back, stiff as lumber. Reverend Swenson had had the foresight to bring rope, so they tied him down real good.

Sam looked at the reverend. "Take him by the missus first, so she can say good-bye?"

"Not with the boy there. Let her do it privately, in town."

Yep, Jeremiah liked this minister more and more. The man cared. To Jeremiah, that was the most important thing a man could do. Mr. Stubb had cared enough to invest in a worthless kid. That kid's own pa hadn't.

One of the things Jeremiah did for Mr. Stubb was to look around where cattle might have been rustled and try to get an idea of what happened. They'd caught three or four rustlers that way. The three men were waiting on him, he knew, but he started looking the area over good. He wanted to know. No tracks, of course. Any tracks were snowed under, not to be found. But the wagon frame told him some things.

The reverend asked, "Why did the robbers that fell upon him and stole his supplies not just take the wagon?"

"'Zactly what I was wonderin' myself." Jeremiah pointed to the near rear hub and axle. "Look close here. You expect it to be black from axle grease like the other hubs. But this black is different. It's charred." He gripped the wheel rim and strained mightily. Wouldn't budge.

Sam nodded. "His wheel wasn't greased enough, and it locked up. Quit turning. Probably smoking, so he had to stop. Pretty smart, Jennings."

Jeremiah pointed. "The off rear wheel is gone. He likely took it off. If I was out here and a wheel locked up, I'd pull the other wheels to steal some grease from each of them and get the bad wheel working again. Reckon that's what he was doing as well."

The reverend nodded. "Good surmise, Mr. Jennings. And if the pneumonia was upon him, he might have been too sick and weak to do much more than clear a spot and build a fire."

Sam said, "Cray Sheets at the hotel says Stedman stayed in town a week. Said he wanted to get back, but he was feeling poorly. Didn't think it was pneumonia though. Just blowing his nose and such. 'Sides, there was that bad storm to delay him, too."

The picture was coming clear. "He delayed in town, trying to feel better, and finally decided he had to get home. Maybe ran out of money; it's expensive staying in town. So he started out, got this far—too far to turn back—and his wheel locked up. And then the pneumonia came on him. And then the robbers. They couldn't move the wagon either, what with that wheel, so they left it and just took his supplies." Jeremiah shook his head. "Everything in the world went bad on him all at once."

Marcus sighed. "And he was such a good man, too."

" 'He sends His rain on the just and the unjust.' Matthew 5 something," Sam quoted.

"Matthew 5:45, I believe. Near the end of that chapter." The reverend took one last look at the forlorn wagon frame and climbed up into his sleigh. "Mr. Jennings, you may come into town with us if you wish, or return to tell the missus what we're doing here. I will take the remains in and then come visit her."

He pondered a moment. "Can the church give the missus a loan? I could get her some supplies."

Sam smiled. "I can spare a dollar or two."

"Me, too," said Marcus.

The reverend bobbed his head and twisted his horse aside to break his runners loose. "Excellent plan." He clucked his horse forward. "Mr. Jennings, you know pretty much what they need most. If you come with us, we'll load up this sleigh for the drive back to

LAURAINE SNELLING

the Stedman place. We're not a wealthy church; in fact, most of us are poor as church mice, so to speak, so we cannot replace the stolen supplies. But we can ease her burden."

"Reverend Swenson, I'm much obliged to you."

Sam said, "And send some more out later, maybe."

Marcus added, "And axle grease. Lots of axle grease."

53

CHAPTER 11

Reverend said he would be out to visit you today." Jeremiah set the milk bucket on the table.

Belle nodded. "Thank you."

"Said he had a niece who was a bit of a handful. Twelve years old, and her parents are at the end of their patience with her."

"That's sad. Is she in trouble? With others, I mean."

"Not that he said—more high-spirited, it sounds like."

"Breakfast is ready. Give Abel a shake, please."

At the prompting, Abel climbed out of bed and shoved his feet into his boots then sat down at the table, still rubbing his eyes. Blue eyes widened when his mother set scrambled eggs with meat in them on the table. "Eggs!"

"I wish there were more, but at least we can enjoy a treat."

Jeremiah inhaled. "Smells like a corner of heaven."

She set a plate of cornmeal patties on the table, too. "One of these days I will make biscuits, but these will do for now." She sat down and smiled at her son. "How would you like to say grace, Abel?"

He nodded. "Thank You, Jesus, for food and milk and Nosey and eggs and that that mean old rooster missed me yesterday. Amen." His words had run into one long one, except for the *amen*, making his mother smile.

When they finished eating, Belle poured more oat coffee into their cups, filling Abel's with cream and then passing the pitcher to Jeremiah. "Cream makes even this kind of coffee palatable."

"It's hot and tastes fine to me."

Rusty scrambled up, his tail wagging on his way to the door where, nose to the edge, he announced they had company coming.

Abel jumped up and retrieved the rifle from the corner, handing it to his mother. When the knock came, he went to open it.

Belle caught Jeremiah's quizzical expression. "Anson insisted after we had an unwelcome visitor one time."

"Ma, it's Reverend Swenson."

"Well, invite him in."

Before the man stepped through the door, Belle put the rifle behind her skirts. "Welcome, Reverend. You're out early."

"Good morning. And a fine morning it is." He nodded to the young girl beside him. "I brought Cordellia along with me, my niece."

"Welcome, Cordellia, I'm Mrs. Stedman. My son, Abel. Our guest, Mr. Jennings. We have some roasted oats coffee if you would like a cup."

"Thank you. We have a few supplies along. Families donated some." He looked to Jeremiah. "And Sam decided he could loan you his old mule. He's getting kind of old for plowing and such, but he was hoping you might find a use for him in case you needed to go for help." He unwound his muffler from around his neck.

"I'll bring the things in." Jeremiah rose and grabbed his coat.

Belle smiled at the gangly girl. "Come sit over here."

Cordellia shook her head. "I'll go help Mr. Jennings if you don't mind."

When the two had left, the reverend took Jeremiah's chair. "I have a big favor to ask. Might you be willing to help us out by keeping Cordellia out here with you for a while? I know she can be a big help, and perhaps you can be a good influence on her. Her ma says she is a real good worker but tends to daydream a lot and has no interest in ladylike pursuits."

Thoughts darted through her mind like spring swallows on a bug hunt. The girl's blue eyes already haunted her. With freckles dusting a turned-up nose, Cordellia could not be called beautiful by any means, but since when did that matter? "We don't have a lot of room, as you know."

"She could sleep in the lean-to or on a pallet on the floor. Her ma said she could send out some flour and such in return for keeping her. Cordellia and your Abel here ought to get along right well."

"What about school? Shouldn't she be in school?"

"Well, I thought as how you can read and write and do sums, mayhap you would teach her." He dropped his voice. "She was the instigator behind several pranks at the schoolhouse, and she and the teacher don't get along too well."

Belle hid a grin. This girl sounded just like her younger sister. Leaving Amy behind was one of the hardest things she had ever done when she and Anson came west. Taking a deep breath, she nodded. "Of course she can stay with us. And while I think there might be a bit of conniving between you and Mr. Jennings, I do believe this will work out for all of us. Far better that she comes here than we get hauled off to stay with someone else."

"God does indeed provide."

The door opened, and Cordellia and Mr. Jennings entered, arms full of supplies, with Rusty dancing at their feet.

"Oh Reverend, how can I ever thank you?"

"It weren't me but the folks of our congregation. When they heard your supplies were stolen, they dug deep."

"How can I repay them?"

"By being a saving grace for Cordellia. With the mule, you'll be able to come to town for church one Sunday in the near future.

Soon's we can bust your wagon out of the ice lock, we'll get it fixed and bring it back for you."

Belle sniffed then had to dab at her eyes.

"You got enough hay for both the cow and the mule?"

"I hope so."

He leaned forward. "Now I hate to get too personal, but do you have any cash on hand?"

She shook her head. "Anson took it all to buy supplies."

"Figured as much. Don't you go getting worried. God will provide, but you got to be honest with me and be willing to ask for help. Now I know that comes hard, but our Father gives us each other to make the road easier. Some people have a need to help, and if you don't ask, you cheat them out of doing what God is telling them to do."

Belle set the cradle to rocking with one foot. "All I can say is thank you."

"Thank Him, not just us."

Cordellia and Jeremiah set the last of the supplies on the floor. "That does it," Jeremiah said.

"Did you bring your things in?" Reverend Swenson asked the girl.

"No, but I will." She looked to Belle. "Are you sure, ma'am?" She glanced down, and her eye caught the cradle. "You have a baby?" Her voice wore awe like a coating of cream.

"Angel was born on Christmas Eve."

"Oh, I love babies. Can I touch her?"

"Of course."

Cordellia knelt by the cradle. "She is so beautiful. And you called her Angel."

"The man told me that was her name." Abel glanced at his mother as if asking if all was well.

"Really, what man?"

"We'll tell you the story later." Belle watched the girl. "Have you been around babies before?"

"Not for a long time." She rose. "I'll go get my things."

"Well, if that is all settled, I'd best be on my way. Jeremiah, you want to take that mule out to the barn? By the way, his name is Samson. Cordellia already made friends with him. The bridle stays with him."

"I cannot say thank you enough," Belle said. "And thank all those generous people for me, too."

"We'll get that wagon back for you as soon as we can. Don't want to leave it there too long, or it will walk off, too." He settled his hat on his head and stepped into the sleigh. "Lord bless and keep you." He clucked at the horse then stopped. "You tell Jeremiah that when he comes back through this way, he's already got family and friends here."

"I will." Belle waved him off and returned to the house, Cordellia right beside her.

"I'll help you put those supplies away."

"Thank you, I just have to figure where to put them all. Soon's the winter weather lets up, we can move the cow and chickens back out to the barn." She turned to the girl. "Do you know how to milk a cow?"

"Yes. I don't care much for chickens. They seem so flighty." She turned at the first whimper from the cradle. "Can I pick her up?"

Belle almost said no, but the look of pleading on the girl's face made her change her mind. "I take it you've been with babies before, then?"

"Like I said, not for a long time. I'll be careful. I promise."

Angel whimpered. Cordellia leaned over the cradle and gently, as if touching thistle down, slid her hands under the wrapped bundle of baby and held her in one arm against her chest. "Angel is such a perfect name for you." She rocked as if it were the most natural thing in the world. "You think it's time to eat?" Cordellia looked up to Belle, her eyes shining. "Thank you."

"I'll show you where to put some of those things while I change her and feed her." Belle did as she said and made herself and the baby comfortable in the rocker. "Abel went out to the barn?"

"I guess so." Cordellia opened each of the packets and filled the tins. "Mrs. March sent you some of her hundred-year sourdough starter. And some flour so you can keep it going. Someone else sent flour, too. Look here." She sniffed a can with a lid. "Someone sent bacon drippings. Now that's strange."

"No, that is wonderful. I can put it in so many things. Soon we'll have butter, too. Such riches." Belle blew out a breath. Now if only Jeremiah didn't have to leave, but she knew he would probably head out tomorrow.

That night Cordellia laid her pallet at the foot of the rope-strung bed, and both she and Abel were asleep within minutes. Jeremiah and Belle, she with the baby sleeping in her arms, sat in front of the fire. Jeremiah had a piece of wood he was carving on, brushing the chips into a pile.

"I meant what I said, you know."

"What—that you're leaving first thing in the morning?"

"Well, that too, but I have given this plenty of thought, and I do believe that I love you. The big question is, do you think you could come to love me?"

The words wanted to leap out of her mouth, but she bade her tongue and lips behave. "It is too soon yet."

"That wasn't the question."

"Oh." She rocked a couple of times, heaving a sigh. "But there are problems, you see."

"Such as?"

"I want to live here, and you will be living on a ranch way northwest of here."

"If you believe you can come to love me, then somehow that will work out." He scraped some chips unto the growing stack. "If I write to you, will you write to me?"

"Yes." There was no hesitation there.

"Good."

"When will you come back?"

"Not until after calving and branding and clearing whatever messes await me. So probably not before June. I will write to you." He dusted off his carving and handed her a wooden horse. "This is the first horse I will give Abel, but not the last." He brushed the shavings pile into a bag he kept handy for tinder.

"I have a feeling Cordellia is going to like it here." He nodded, thinking as he stared into the fire. "I think God sent her."

"Like He sent you?" She had a hard time believing she'd said that, but so truly God had been guiding Jeremiah.

"Maybe you can trade butter and cheese for hay or grain when you need it. Your wagon will take some fixin'."

"Are you sure you meant … ah, meant what you said?" Her heart felt like it might leap out of her mouth.

"That I love you?"

"Yes." She let the words nestle around her heart.

"Guess it gets easier with the saying."

"I guess."

He rose and leaned over, tipping her chin up with one finger. "And this is what love feels like."

His kiss not only warmed her lips but her heart and traveled deep into her soul. When he lifted his mouth, she let her head rest on the back of the rocker, staring up at him with seeking eyes.

"I will see you in June."

The next morning, his words echoed in her heart as she and Abel, along with Cordellia, waved him good-bye. They stood in front of the sod house, sun glinting on the snow, and waved until they couldn't see him. "The Lord keep thee safe," she whispered. Jeremiah's words, *All will be well,* echoed again in her heart. "Please Lord, let that be so."

EPILOGUE

You sure he will be here?" Cordellia asked with a skeptical look from under her brows.

"He said he would be." And he's never lied yet. Belle breathed a silent prayer. The last time someone didn't come home when he said was when Anson didn't return, and it wasn't his fault. *Dear Lord, not again, please.*

Abel burst into the room. "He's here! He's here!"

Belle felt her knees near to buckle. Relief could cause that, same as fear. *Thank You, Lord. You got me through before; thank You for now.* Every morning she woke with *thank You* on her mind. Thank You burst in like the first green grass and the meadowlarks singing. All were announcing they were back. The prairie was no longer locked in winter. She started for the door, and Mrs. Swenson grabbed her arm.

"It's bad luck to see the groom on your wedding day before the ceremony, a'course."

"All right, if you insist, but can I send him a message?"

The two women in the room with her looked at each other and shrugged.

Cordellia, eyes shining, announced, "I'll go tell him."

"Tell him ..." Belle closed her eyes. "Tell him all is well."

"That all?"

"Yes, that is all." She'd signed the letter almost that way, only "All will be well." And he'd answered. Letters had been her lifeline in the months since that day after Christmas when he'd ridden north to his new job.

She returned in a minute. "You shoulda seen his face—like the sun lit it."

Belle felt peace settle over her. She looked over to the corner where one of her friends had picked up the baby. At five months, Angel charmed everyone.

A knock at the door, and Reverend Swenson asked, "You ready?"

"Yes." Belle picked up her bouquet of pink prairie roses, one of her favorite spring and summer flowers, and Cordellia, carrying Angel, walked out first. Belle followed her and paused at the door. Abel stepped in beside her and grinned up at her.

"He's up front." His whisper could have carried clear to Fargo.

Belle nodded.

The man to the right of the reverend turned with a smile that encompassed his entire face.

At the reverend's slight nod, a woman started to sing. "Holy, holy, holy, Lord God Almighty."

Belle repeated her vows to love, honor, and obey with a firm voice, looking into eyes that searched clear to her soul.

Angel chortled from the front row. Abel snickered, and a titter ran through those present. This was too special an occasion not to smile and rejoice.

"You may kiss your bride." Belle floated into Jeremiah's arms and heard Angel again. Angels singing? How appropriate. With her cowboy at her side, Belle took the first step in the journey to her new life. And all would be well, for the God who had brought them together and guided them to this point would never leave. When Reverend Swenson gave the blessing, everyone said, "Amen." And Angel, who had stolen the cowboy's heart at their first meeting, chortled again.